Let's Find Out About
Bicycles

by Mary Ebeltoft Reid   **Photographs by Scott Goldsmith**

LET'S FIND OUT
LIBRARY

Scholastic Inc.
New York   Toronto   London   Auckland   Sydney

We are grateful to the Cannondale Corporation for the opportunity to photograph this book at their Bedford, Pennsylvania, factory and especially to Mark Diehl for his generous help. Special thanks to William's Circle Cycle in Hicksville, N.Y.

Photographs by Scott Goldsmith
Cover photograph by James Levin
Illustrations by Barbara Gray
Design by Alleycat Design

1 2 3 4 5 6 7 8 9 10   02 01 00 99 98 97 96

Bicycles are fun!
How are they made?
Let's find out.

3

Bike tires are made of rubber.
Rubber comes from trees in the rain forest.

Steel or aluminum is used to make bike frames.
Steel comes from rocks called iron ore.

JACK VAN ANTWERP/ THE STOCK MARKET

At the steel mill, the ore is heated until the iron melts!
Carbon is mixed with the hot iron to make steel.

The metal is shaped into pipes at the pipe mill.

At the bicycle factory, workers cut the pipes. They cut just the right sizes for making bikes!

Then a laser beam cuts holes in the pipe pieces.
This man uses a computer to program the laser.

The pipes are used to make the bike frame. They fit together like a jigsaw puzzle. A welder fastens them with a welding torch.

Workers in this factory sand the welds to make them smooth.

This woman inspects the frame. She wears glasses
and a mask to protect her from metal dust.

It's time to paint! The bike frames move slowly on a conveyor. The painter sprays each frame. Today he is using Speed Yellow.

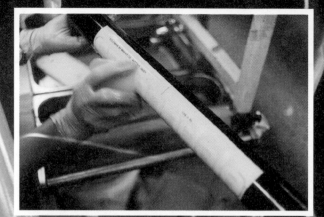

The painter wears boots, coveralls, and a helmet to protect his clothes and eyes. When the frames are dry, other workers add labels.

Now for the wheels! The metal hubs and spokes come from another factory. This woman puts spokes into a round wheel rim.

A robot tests the wheels to make sure they don't wobble. Then a worker adds the sprocket.

Another worker adds an inner tube and a rubber tire.
She pumps air into the tube.

Packers pack the frames, handlebars, and seats
for shipping. The wheels go into another box.
The bikes will be put together at the store.

A factory like this one can make up to 800 bikes a day! The frames and wheels are shipped from the warehouse.

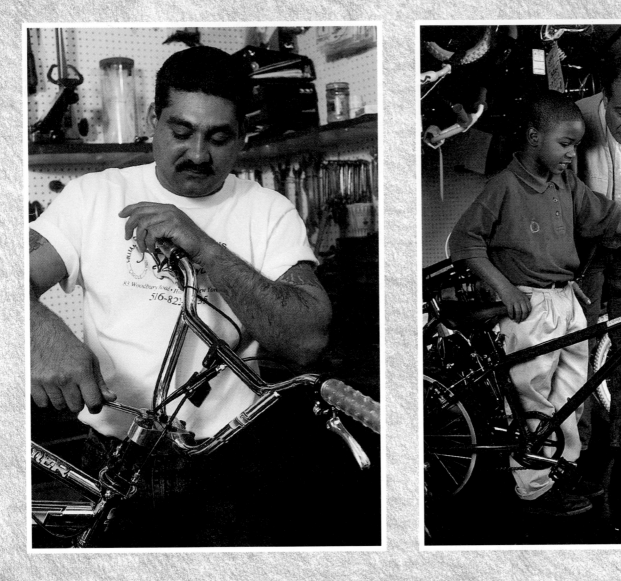

At the store, a worker uses tools to put each bike together. The owner helps a customer choose one.

This customer has found
just the right bike.
Off she goes!

Let's Find Out About
Bicycles!

Iron ore

Steel mill

PIPE FACTORY

SPEEDY BICYCLE FACTORY

Trailer truck

Hand truck

Welder

Weld sander

Inspe

Conveyor belt

Laser

Computer

Painter

Pipe cutter

Labeler

22

Adding sprocket

Inner tubes & tires

YAY!

ACE CYCLE SHOP

We're Open

Robot

SPEEDY BICYCLE FACTORY

WHEELS

Rims and Spokes

Packers

Warehouse

Forklift

23

For Grown-Ups

We hope you have fun with this book! Here are some things to do as you read and enjoy it together.

Before reading, talk about different kinds of bicycles: 3-speed, 10-speed, mountain bikes, bikes with training wheels, racing bikes. Then name parts of a bike, such as the handlebars, frame, tires, and pedals. "What do you think they are made from? Do all bikes have them?" Children will observe bicycles more closely than ever before!

Read and reread! Read once through the whole story. Then reread, taking time to look closely at each picture and talk about it.

Retell the sequence of making bikes. Use the illustration on pages 22-23 to help you tell the story.

Talk about the jobs the workers do, and the clothes and equipment they use. Which job would you like to do?

Pretend! Pretend you are workers in a bicycle factory. Dramatize the actions of the workers. Make the sounds of machines. Pretend you are welding metal tubes into a frame, or painting bike frames that move along on a conveyor belt.